# MRS HONEY HOLIDAY

## written and illustrated
## by Pam Adams

### Child's Play (International) Ltd
Swindon     New York     Bologna

© 1992 Pam Adams    ISBN 0-85953-755-2 (hard cover)    Printed in Singapore
ISBN 0-85953-756-0 (soft cover)

Mrs Honey needed a rest.

She decided to go away
for a few days
with her grandchildren.

On the plane,
they ate lunch
from little plastic trays.

Early next morning,
they looked out
of the window
of their hotel room.

In the square below,
some children
were skate-boarding.

"I wish I could do that,"
sighed Peter.

"When I was a girl,
I used to roller skate,"
said Mrs Honey.

"I was rather good at it.
It must be much the same
as skate-boarding.

"You can do anything if you try!"

Mrs Honey imagined herself skate-boarding.

The children imagined Mrs Honey
skate-boarding.

So, they decided to try.
And it was fun.

Afterwards, they went to the pool.
A girl was diving
from the high board.

"I wish I could dive like that,"
sighed Emma.

"I'd be scared," said Peter.

"I used to dive,"
said Mrs Honey.
"I won lots of trophies.

"You can do anything if you try!"

Mrs Honey
imagined herself
diving.

The children imagined
Mrs Honey diving.

So, they tried. And it was fun.

Next day, they had a picnic.

Some children were riding ponies.

"I wish I could ride,"
said Peter.

"Me, too, but I might fall off,"
said Emma.

"I used to ride superbly,"
said Mrs Honey.

"You can do anything if you try!"

Mrs Honey imagined herself riding.

The children imagined Mrs Honey riding.

So they tried. And it was fun.

That evening, there was music and dancing.

"I wish I could play the guitar," said Peter.

"I wish I could dance like that," said Emma.

"I won a prize for dancing," said Mrs Honey.

"You can do anything if you try!"

Mrs Honey imagined herself dancing.

The children
imagined
Mrs Honey
dancing.

So, they tried.
And they both
learned a lot.

Next day,
there was a regatta.
Two boats were racing.

"I wish I could row like that,"
said Peter.

"I used to row," said Mrs Honey.
"And I won many races.

"You can do anything if you try!"

"Oh goody!
We can go out in a boat,"
cried Emma.

"And you can show us
how you did it, Granny,"
added Peter.

So Mrs Honey tried...

And the children
thought it was fun.

The next morning,
Mrs Honey and the children
were invited to go on a boat trip.
Some people were deep sea diving.

"It looks deep," said Peter.
"But I am sure we can learn.
You can do anything, if you try!"

"I have a bit of a cold, today,"
said Mrs Honey.
"Perhaps, next time."

Mrs Honey and the children imagined themselves diving.

The holiday was nearly over.
It was time to pack.

"We seem to have more things
to take home than we had
when we arrived,"
said Mrs Honey.

"Never mind.
We'll get everything in somehow."

"You can do anything, if you try!"
laughed the children.

The children were looking forward
to being home.

"We can't wait to try
all the things we've learned."

Mrs Honey was looking forward
to being home, too.

"What I need is a good rest,"
she thought.